The Deliverance
of Dancing Bears

To Gordon

The Deliverance of Dancing Bears

Elizabeth Stanley

Kane/Miller
BOOK PUBLISHERS

First American Edition 2003 by Kane/Miller Book Publishers
La Jolla, California

First published in 1994 by the University of Western Australia Press
Nedlands, Western Australia 6009, under the Cygnet Books imprint.

Kane/Miller Book Publishers
P.O. Box 8515
La Jolla, CA 92038
www.kanemiller.com

Library of Congress Control Number: 2002112322

Printed and bound in Singapore by Tien Wah Press (Pte.), Ltd.

1 2 3 4 5 6 7 8 9 10

ISBN 1-929132-41-7

Hope is a waking dream

Aristotle

HERE was once a large, brown bear who dreamed of a different life.

A life of wandering in the forests, of drinking the cool, clear water of mountain streams, of eating there, with her partner, in the shallows, where the fish paused to rest amongst the smooth, green rocks beneath the surface.

AND lying lazily in the sun with her babies, as they climbed over her and licked her big brown face. A life of peace and freedom.

O make these dreams, the bear had to close her eyes to the bars of the iron cage in which she lived.

To lift the thrashing, shining fish from the stream of her dreams, she had to fold her legs beneath her great body so that she could forget her sharp claws had long since been cut, and stunted.

The babies of her dreams nuzzled up to a warm, wet nose, which was not shackled with the hard iron ring she now wore, night and day.

And so she spent most of her life curled into herself, eyes closed, wandering the forests of her mind.

BUT these dreams were regularly broken by Halûk, her keeper, who came clattering at the door of her cage, shouting and swearing and smashing his long, wooden rod against the iron bars that surrounded the bear.

Halûk was full of anger and hatred, and he terrified the bear. She was so afraid of his wrath and cruelty that she would have lashed out at him in defense, had he not blunted her claws and sawn off her powerful teeth.

Instead, she succumbed fearfully to the heavy chain latched to her ringed nose, and to the sting of the rod she felt across her back, as she was wrenched out of the refuge of her cage.

ACH day, Halûk took her to the market square where he made her dance to amuse the people gathered there. Around and around the poor bear turned on her two back legs, her head pulled from side to side by the chain which Halûk jangled to the clatter of his tambourine.

People stopped and stared and sometimes threw coins into the hat, which he had tossed on the ground at the bear's feet.

This performance continued relentlessly for many hours until the day began to fade, the stalls closed, and the people went home. Then, Halûk would lead the bear back to her cage and lock the door.

It was always the same, the dancing by day and then the dreaming.

Halûk never understood that it was the dreaming and not the bread and water he left each evening that kept the bear living, year after year.

NE day, an old man followed
Halûk back from the market
square where the bear had been dancing.

"What do you want for this dancing
bear?" asked the man.

Halûk looked at him suspiciously.

"More than you would be willing to
pay!" he shouted.

"Name your price," replied the stranger.

ALÛK was paid a large sum of money over which he gloated greedily as he hurried away, leaving the old man named Yusuf holding the bear by the chain which hung from her nose.

"How often have I watched you, poor beast, dancing humiliated in the market square on this loathsome chain," he said. "I've dreamed of you wandering in the forests where you belong, and fishing the mountain streams. I feel too ashamed to have you dancing another day. I have no way of returning you to your home and your loved ones, but come with me, and I will restore to you a little happiness."

AND so, Yusuf took the bear home to where he lived alone in a humble cottage by a wood, outside of the town.

Beyond the cottage, running down to a small stream, was a lush garden of long green grass and shady trees. Yusuf led the bear into the garden and down to the stream, where she dropped into the soft grass and plunged her shackled nose deep into the water to drink.

Yusuf began to stroke her big, soft head as she drank, but the poor creature cowered at his touch, and her eyes widened in terror when he drew close to her. The old man wept; he understood the depth of her suffering.

Taking the iron ring from her nose, he caressed her reassuringly. Then, leaving her to discover the tranquility of his lovely garden, he carefully prepared for her a restful sleeping place under the shelter of the trees.

URING the weeks that followed, Yusuf cared for the bear with tenderness and compassion. She began to trust him. In the afternoons, they sat under the trees by the stream and dreamed together. In the evenings, he would feed her generously and leave her to sleep.

One morning, many months later, Yusuf came into the marketplace to buy a donkey. The frail old man found a crowd milling beneath the clock tower. It took him some time to press his way through the throng of people to discover what was drawing their interest.

Aghast, he came upon the gypsy Halûk, flaunting a small bear cub and forcing him upright onto two legs with the wrench of the chain which held his tender snout. Halûk's wooden staff cracked mercilessly across the nose of the little bear, when he dropped whimpering to the ground, exhausted and confused by his unfamiliar and painful harness. The crowd looked on with dumb curiosity.

"AH, look who is here, the madman who would squander his savings for a stupid beast," scorned Halûk, as he caught sight of Yusuf straining forward through the crowd.

"Old man, where is your bear? Have you lost her? Have you come to buy another?" he taunted.

The people stared at Yusuf in silence. His savings for a much needed donkey were in his pocket.

"Yes," he said quietly, "the same price again."

He held out a fist full of notes to Halûk, who snatched the money without hesitation.

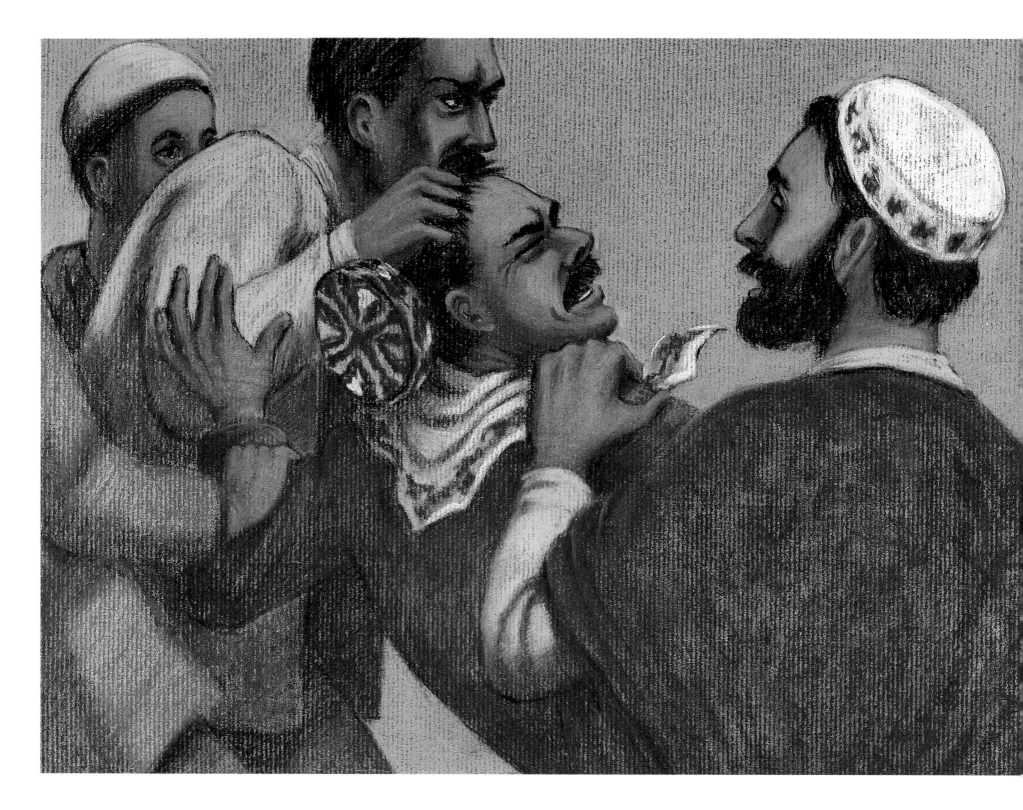

 OUNDS of protest began to break from the watching crowd. "Halûk, you are a tyrant to take the old man's money. It is surely all he has," accused one man.

"You must give it back, Halûk. The man is old and already poor," demanded another.

Halûk had the money securely in his coat pocket and was pushing defiantly against the crowd which would not let him pass.

Yusuf thrust his hand into the air and called out, "Please stop! Please let him go!" But a young man insisted, "Yusuf, he has robbed you! It is too much to pay for the wretched bear!" He had Halûk by the hair and held him relentlessly.

"NO!" replied Yusuf. He took up the chain, which restrained the small and miserable bear, and tended the bleeding muzzle.

"Sometimes one must pay a high price for a different life, for a life one has dreamed of," he said, stroking the bear.

The peace he could now share with this tormented young creature seemed a fitting kind of restitution at the end of his own long life of struggle and sacrifice.

"You good people have at last spurned this man for his performing bears. Halûk will pay a high price for his shame. But now, he too has the chance to dream of something different."

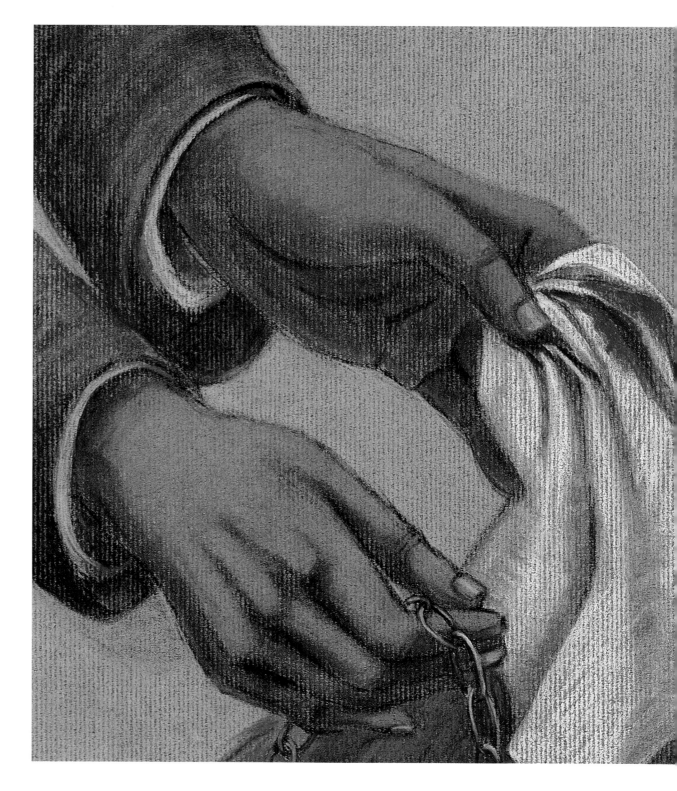

HE people released Halûk, who fell to the ground. Humbled by Yusuf's words, he watched silently as the old man and the bear walked home together to the little cottage by the wood.

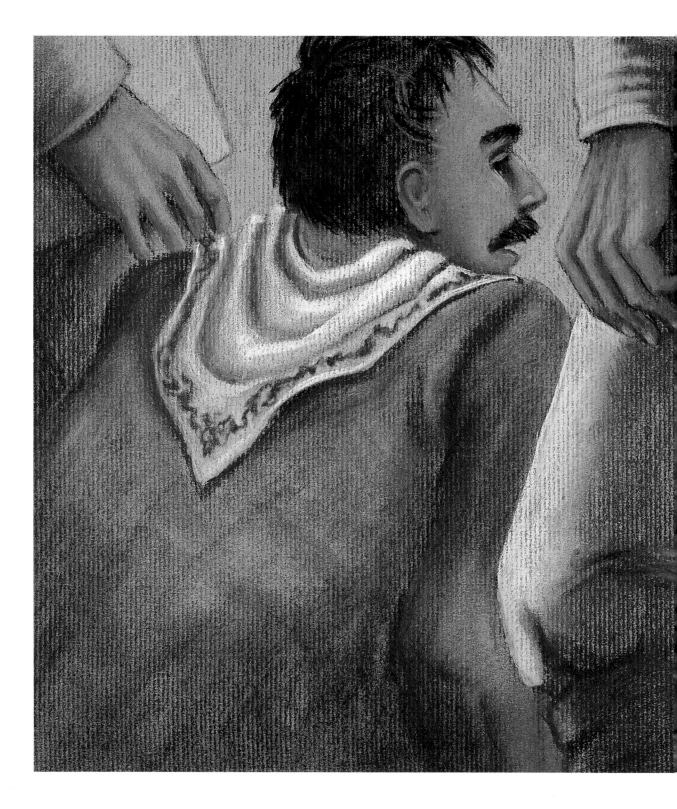

Postscript

I saw my first dancing bear in Athens in 1979. That experience remained vivid and painful in my memory for years afterwards until I was able to "lay the ghost," as it were, by writing this fable.

The original story was written well in advance of the illustrations, though many changes followed up to, and during, the making of the pictures. My research for the illustrations led me to focus on Turkey as the setting for the story. For in this country, the practice of dancing, captive bears, though unlawful, was still thriving. There was growing concern for the poor image it established amongst the increasing numbers of tourists, and for the serious depletion of the bear population in Turkey's mountainous regions, where the animals were relentlessly hunted.

I therefore decided to travel to Turkey in October 1993, with some expectation that I might again witness this unhappy dance somewhere in Istanbul, or perhaps along the tourist routes on the Aegean. Chiefly, I wanted to collect visual information with sketchbook and camera of the country itself, its landscape, its architecture, the people and their lifestyle.

I had not dreamed that these modest travel plans would become, for me, a kind of pilgrimage, during which the responsibility I felt that I (and all mankind) carried for the continuing abuse of these great creatures was miraculously absolved.

On the day I arrived in Istanbul, I discovered that the bears I had come to witness as captives had, in fact, been liberated the night before! Since 1992, and unbeknownst to me, the World Society for the Protection of Animals had been working with the Turkish government towards this wonderful climax. Rescued dramatically overnight from the long-term abuse and neglect of their gypsy keepers, twelve of these bears were rushed, anaesthetized, to the refuge of the Uludag University in Bursa, where their health and welfare was to be closely monitored in specially constructed compounds in the Veterinary Department. They were to be released into a ten-hectare sanctuary forest, where they would be fed and cared for by rangers for the rest of their lives. The hope was that some would be able to breed there, and that future cubs might be returned to the wild.

My story is about the power of dreams. That captive bears no longer dance in the streets of Turkey and Greece, vindicates this story.

For more information on the salvation of captive bears and other abused animals throughout the world, contact:

WSPA USA
34 Deloss Street
Framingham, MA 01702   USA

Phone: +1 508 879 8350
Fax: +1 508 620 0786

E-mail: wspa@wspausa.com
Web: http://www.wspa-usa.org

Dreamers, dream on!
Elizabeth Stanley